THE YELLER BRICK TRAIL

Heaven Knows the Struggling Bit-Player

J'Tone

authorHOUSE®

AuthorHouse™
1663 Liberty Drive
Bloomington, IN 47403
www.authorhouse.com
Phone: 1 (800) 839-8640

Published by AuthorHouse 02/15/2019

ISBN: 978-1-4343-9413-2 (sc)
ISBN: 978-1-4343-9415-6 (hc)
ISBN: 978-1-4343-9414-9 (e)

Library of Congress Control Number: 2008905612

Print information available on the last page.

This book is printed on acid-free paper.

FOREWORD

This light-hearted story follows the fanciful, often ridiculous adventures of two naïve, unseasoned, stumbling, yet likeable entertainers, "The Smenelli brothers." Though born and branded in a remote village in the wildest state in the union, Tony and Joe Smenelli have dreamed since childhood of becoming show-biz stars.

In their attempts to break into the big-time, they often come face to face with celebrities of stage and screen. Their inexperience, haste and innate clumsiness, however, prevent their gaining kinder recognition. In this regard, *The Yeller Brick Trail* might be subtitled *Heaven Knows the Struggling Bit-Player*. But as the main title implies, (with enough Hoot-spa) fortune and possibilities beyond imagination await the worthy venturer.

The Smenelli brothers are destined to represent the legions of lost, straw-legged, nervous, tin-headed hopefuls, including all of us who've ever followed a vision within ourselves and tried to go over the rainbow.

Yet, once you've known their roots, shared in their struggles, examined their hearts, I believe you'll begin encouraging them along with their mom —

"Break your legs, sons," which is to say, "Give them all you got." "They'll love ya for it . . . regardless of all your shortcomings."

"We'll do just that, Ma."

"And God bless everyone back home . . . including ole sour puss Pa."

<u>MUSQUE INSPIRER</u>: POINTE du JOUR, PAR 'RAVEL'S DAPHNIS ET CHLOE.'

<u>DECOR</u>: AERIEN — au MILLEU de ALPAGE/des MONTAGUE/ zu PARADIS MAGNIFIQUE.

AERIAL VANTAGE: In the low light of early morn, we glide silently at first, in low level flight over a misty alpine meadow, within an uncharted mountain wilderness of the Western Rockies. This is not a Western – I reiterate, this is not a Western, even though scenes and elements of cowboy life are oft featured.

Bird song entreats sweetly a mystic, pastoral dawn, followed by the soothing pipes of Indian ghost, mythical faun, or angelic flutist. The sensuous strain of strings (*harp y compris*) are as heaven-sent as is this *sauvage* panorama fete before us. For though we are in time present, this living feast is what precious little remains of God's virginal creation prior to the greedy raping of western expansion.

As we are about to collide head on into a precipice, the majestic music builds ever gently to an erotic intensity and we rise heavenward. The romantic melody rises, then soars as we safely avoid crashing into the huge cliff's rocky crest. Suddenly our vantage view is of an immense breathtaking valley, with still more mountain peaks beyond. We are in total awe, even at times terrified at the crossings of still loftier peaks when we see jagged, incredibly deep canyons and chasms and wild raging rivers below and before, with no place to land in an emergency. Yet, we come away with an overwhelming sense of our magnificent Creator.

—DEMODULATE/diminish soft

Once more, we drift in silence. Ahead, unexpectedly, the canyon range — to where we descend. Heartwarming country western music slowly increases in value and volume as we zoom in on two cheerful young rascals dancing and clowning for momma Scarlet and friends sitting atop hay bales. Add: a few fiddlers, people clapping, stomping, clogging, laughing, hooting and hollering. (Seen briefly on a fly by)

Home on the Range

A summer day, Hicksville, Idaho. This remote mountain village is known possessively only to a few dreamy-eyed romantics and the most ardent of golden trout fishermen. But, occasionally, a rugged film crew will venture here to shoot its majestic mountain skyscapes.

Their wide-angle lenses will eventually tilt down past tall spruce, golden aspen and broad maples to where goat and cattle graze on a hillside left in purple columbine and other native pasture. Meanwhile, just off camera, audio technicians will be out gathering bird songs to add later to the final mix.

Further down this broad landscape is Cannon Range and the Smenelli Beefalow Ranch. Several crumbling farm buildings surrounded by rolling fields of alfalfa ready for second cutting. Nestled among flowering bush, shrubs and forgotten farm implements lies a rustic ranch house of log and stone. A cast iron stewer and an old oaken bucket hung from an ancient box pump are but a few of the versatile flower pots livening the back porch. All around the house are quaint pleasantries including a potter's wheel, iron castings, a weaver's loom, driftwood, and nature's own peculiarities all rendered priceless by mom's homespun touch.

Further from the house we find the remains of their "Winged Heritage" amid the primeval junkyard of man. A crippled Conestoga wagon, planted where it last got stuck after its hard journey here, is a memorial to great grandpappy who long ago homesteaded here from afar. He came by way of Arkansaw, Tennessee, the Virginie Coast, Italia, dust, a dream and a destined star.

Further on, a busted child's go cart, rusted scythe,

3

oxen yoke, bicycle parts and other historic discards decorate the weed lawn around the crumbling goat shed.

Behind the goat shed, two primary school-age boys (the budding Smenelli brothers, Tony and Joe) laugh and jiggle clumsily atop a humongous Douglas Fir stump. Their dog, Scamp, dancing and dodging about, tries to muscle in on their act by hopping on and off again and again. About a dozen or so odd kids, who were also trying to stay on the stump, are kicked off one by one until only the two young wild west lads are left.

Lounging on one of the hay bales nearby, Scarlet (their ex-show gal, mom) absently teases her flaming-red hair, while smiling proudly at the amusing antics of her two energetic show-offs: six-year-old Tony and Joey, her eldest.

After a few moments, Barrb-wire Smenelli (Tony and Joe's tough, no-nonsense, anti-show-biz pa) gallops up angrily on Wildfire and chases his sons back to their chores.

*   *   *   *

Night falls. Rodeo prizes and prints, Shoshone Indian artifacts and other Western décor flavor the rustic family room of the Smenelli ranch house.

While Barrb tells a manly tale of pioneering heyday, his sons (in Indian costume and war paint) wait eagerly with authentic bows and tomahawks to act out his yarn. Then with all the hoot and holler of a wild-west show, Barrb chases his two chuckling sons about the house and in turn is pursued by Scamp.

Barrb: Giddy-Yup, Wildfire! Let's get them their savages! Scarlet, get this dang dog.... Hey! They're getting away! Yippee-ki-yaah-ki-yon-away!

Scarlet, pretending to join the horseplay, hog ties her yelping mate to the Steinway piano, then promptly leads her rebellious little injuns to the tub.

Left tied to the piano, alone in the dark, Barrb, ever fearless and high spirited, yelps long into the night...with accompaniment from Scamp.

*   *   *   *

Several years have passed. The Smenelli brothers (now in their late teens and a bit more polished) are back by popular demand upon the old stump entertaining proud Scarlet and a gathering of young friends.

Making his usual surprise appearance, Barrb gallops up, Wildfire rises and snorts and a piece of the goat shed is destroyed by a warning gun blast. This promptly disperses the star performers back to their chores, Scamp to beneath the shed and the audience to parts unknown.

*   *   *   *

Months later, in the upper pasture amid a background of dazzling autumnal foliage, the Smenellis are busy repairing a stretch of fence. Though the day is bright and breezy, they appear sullen. Troubled by the loss of closeness he once shared with his wife and sons, Barrb will now attempt a more loving approach.

Barrb:　　　　　　Tony-Boy! Joe-B! Break for lunch,
　　　　　　　　　Boys! Scarlet, set out that their basket
　　　　　　　　　of fancy vittles you prepared up extra
　　　　　　　　　special. Bet you boys can't guess what
　　　　　　　　　favorites your ma put in there? (no
　　　　　　　　　answer)

　　　　　　　　　Yeperoo. Any family head'd be proud
　　　　　　　　　as a twelve-point buck to've been
　　　　　　　　　blessed with a wife and sons like I have
　　　　　　　　　right c'here. Standing up under all this
　　　　　　　　　work and not a squawk or a sass (at
　　　　　　　　　their lack of response). Yeperoo. Nary
　　　　　　　　　a peep.

A picnic lunch is set out upon the coarse buffalo grass.
Barrb touches his sons' shoulders, nods and they bow
their heads to pray. After thanking the Lord, they begin
eating.

With the poetic manner of a plain parson, Barrb
compares the virtues of the good country life to the
pitfalls encountered by fools venturing to Sin City. Joe
respectfully raises his hand.

Joe:　　　　　　　Might I speak freely on that
　　　　　　　　　subject, Pa?

Barrb:　　　　　　You know right well you might,
　　　　　　　　　my boy.

After glancing at his brother and mom for support, Joe
clears his throat.

Joe: I listened real good to all you had to say, Pa. (deep breath) But when I recalls falling off my dumb, bowlegged mare what got me ankle busted in a cantankerous gopher hole and tramped on by a multitude of highly ignorant pregnant cows who surely know'd me as the fool they see mucking out their stalls in my Sundays, an' you know'n how I cried leading my cute calf Thelma to that there butcher. Lord, I know where Hell is. It's down there'n that smelly, festered ole' slaughter pit when it's my turn to honey dip it out emptying rat traps 'fore breakfast. (sigh) All that sure ain't my idea of the good life, Pa.

Barrb: Darn, Joe-B! I can't never tell stew from fricassee in what you say, Boy. Scarlet, you any notion what this big goof of yours been sputtering?

Scarlet: It appears he...

Joe: You see Pa, I...

Barrb: Hush up! Seems the second I'm sweet tempered, some scheming back shooter takes advantage. Way he puts it, ain't no slime, rats, spit, nor slaughter pits 'hind all them shiny city lights, nor, some of the ugliest, most ignorant animules on earth (demonstrating) sashaying down them bright boulevards.

Scarlet: Add quicksand and earthquakes, they'd still fight to go.

Barrb: Go where – on their merry way to hard times?

Scarlet: Haven't you found that hard times can be blessings, too?

Barrb: Did we?

Tony: Pa, you know how me and Joe-B been hankering to tangle into show-biz?

Joe: We're sorta preparing to go soon, Pa.

Barrb: How soon?

Scarlet: They're nearly grown men, Barrb.

Joe: Even got me a touch a' arthritis right c'here 'n my back.

Barrb: Joe-B, your back's stronger 'n...

Tony: Not even Grand-Pappy Williams lived old 'nough to get it in the back.

Barrb: Then maybe we'll just shoot ole Joe and put him out of...

Tony/Joe: What you say, Pa? You gonna let us go?

Barrb: Well, I – ya....

(Drawn by cattle moans, Barrb see his cattle escaping through an open fence.)

Barrb:	Hey!!! Now you did it. There goes Tootsie leading them out again, shaking their tails like them there shameless go-go dancers. If'n we don't round them up quick, they'll be partying all over the county.
Scarlet/Tony/Joe:	Are you suggesting it's our fault?
Tony/Joe:	We nearly had the fence fixed. And you called us away to chow.
Barrb:	I ya..... (looking at the sun) must be near goat milking time.
Joe:	Goat! What about them go-go cows, Pa?
Barrb:	Ahh, let'em skedaddle for now. Katie and 'er ma'll be by soon to pick up standard and colostrums for their nice little nursery. 'Bout time to milk them damn toggs. Ain't that right Scarlet?
Scarlet:	If you say so, dear. (starts off) My, won't Ms. Prim, Gorgeous and the other girls be surprised to be milked in the glorified light of day?
Barrb:	Hold tight'n your boots, Scarlet. (mounting his horse) Don't dare lower yourself to be doin' so disgraceful a feminee chore as doe maid. Here on out, the boys'll do the milking.
Tony:	Don't you want me and Joe-B to round up them runaways with you, Pa?

Barrb: That's man's work. You choose to be
                     show folk? Start by doing the girlish
                     chores 'round here. (starts to ride off)
                     And Scarlet, cancel that special order
                     for them prize Milner cutting horses.
                     Only surprises in store for your two
                     fools'll be all the troubles waiting
                     out'ch yonder in Witch City! (Barrb
                     whips about and rides off briskly

*   *   *   *

Right about here I might mention that the kids' intention
to go it big in "SHOW BIZ" wasn't solely initiated by their
"ex-show girl" (who swore she almost made it) mom. No
siree Job. Unawares, their big ole bully, de-mandibled Pa
had more'n a lot to do with it. Though he may not be the
world's best to boast how great an athlete, and nearly
met the highest tests in rodeoin', it's a sure bet he could
take the number two spot in Bragadodyoin'.

For it sure weren't sweet tempered, mild-mannered
Scarlet, the sadly aging one-time would-be starlet who
dragged her two young-uns from their violin lessons to get
all trampled-up at the GOOD-OLE CALGARY ROUND-UP.
But there again along with all the blood and getting gored,
sprung the inspiration to entertain plain ole rodeo folk. It
arose each time their admiring girl-fans and feller cow-pokes
rose and gave applause just for falling off some half-broke,
ornery horse. The overwhelming desire to go right back into
that fire and burn their butts was in no small part inspired
by their ole Pa who yelled the loudest and proudest amid
the huge crowd the old family credo of "WE SMENELLIS
WILL NEVER YIELD," while his sons half conscious, bravely
smiled and waved as they were carried off the field.

Neither was it Scarlet who taught the boys the bloody hand-to-feet, head-to-knee combatant contact sports like Americano foota-ball, or the kill-or-be-killed local native style Lacrosse. And here again was the great incentive of audience applause as they were ambulanced from the battle zone.

So in the end, other than the attention from family and friends, they never got diddly-squat for endin' up recuperating on their attic cots half-dead — the credit for these two helpless, innocent rascals' willingness to show off all they wish they were capable of, all they honestly believed they could have achieved if it weren't for . . . something — the full credit for all that can be evenly split twixt their warm, protective, ever-lovin' mother and their "Hoppity-gallopipy-along" 'til-you-drop-dead DAD.

*   *   *   *

The boys' bedroom at sunset. From their bunks, the brothers gaze sadly out at the enormous sun setting slowly beyond an impassible mountain ridge.

Tony:	Joe-B, you suppose that ole show-boat Ma tells of'll ever come sailing over that high and mighty summit to dock at our ole stump out back?
Joe:	Whelp, after our great-grannie folk lighted from Tennessee, didn't they make it all the way out'ch here'n nothing fancier'n a busted down Conestoga powered by a three quarter dead ole ox?
Tony:	Anyhow, that's what ole' Pa said.

Joe: Then there's no reason why Mr. Merrick or any them big production money hustlers can't out do our by gone, crippled ole Grannie and some wobbly knee'd, tongue drooping, castrated ole dead bull.

Tony: I reckon. Wow! Can't you just see it, Joe-B? One night, we'll be gawking out there't that glorious sunset, and by golly, there be coming a boatload of them God-gifted show folk, dancing, rejoicing and floating in to greet us on one of them big, fluffy pinky red and gray purplish clouds.

Joe: Like the good folks did at Pentecost...

Tony: The "Flying Dutchman"...

Joe: Or the great ark that came to rest on the scared mountain of Ararat.

Tony: Coming right for us.

Joe: With heavenly hosts hallowed in colorful lights.

Tony: In grand, hallelujah, Hollywood, "give my regards to Broadway" style.

(Intensely enthused, they cheer and bounce about on their bunks.)

Joe: Boy! Show business is sure more fun than sidestepping meadow muffins and milking dumb ole' goats?

(After sharing a good laugh, Tony sits uneasily.)

Joe: Tony-Boy, you alright?

Tony: I forgot to consider how wide and deep and dangerous be Big Nugget River. But first they gotta cross the Snake and fly over Hanged Ear Canyon, then put up with all them troubled and crying Injun spirits.

Joe: Which requires summing to heart as much gumption as ole Job, I bet. You know I ain't good at figuring things scientific way you do, Ole Bean. What might their chances of getting here alive be?

Tony: (Laying an encouraging hand on Joe's shoulder) Gotta be honest with you Joe-B. The fact is, that big ole canyon's plum sitiated 'bout exactly half a multi-meter tween us right c'here'n the city of New York way out'ch yonder. If my eyesight and calculations are correct, we're sealed off from the entire world here by treacherous rivers, giant pot holes and stone walls like a couple of Chinese teddy bears.

Joe: Must be God's will. We had our own way, we'd a gone to the big city on your happy seventh birthday and right now be so out of place somewhere like two, three-toed socks riding bareback on a disgusted ole penguin.

Tony: (considering) What fool talk was that? You and nobody born alive ain't ever saw such critters. Specially no disgusted ole penguin, what be the happiest, most playful of God's creatures, I know'd.

Joe: Heck, Tony, anybody can get disgusted. Can't you reckon penguins get fed up too being stuck out 'n the middle of nowhere with nothing but fewer and fewerist of raw fish and melting ice burgers to subsist upon, plus frozen feets and hunters in helicopter gunships shooting at you all the time?

Tony: I reckon.

Having worked themselves back into a depression deeper than Hanged Ear Canyon, the imaginative youths return their sad, sleepy stare out beyond the sunset, then listen to a faint distant chorus heralding in their fanciful Show Boat. Since early childhood they've shared many a similar nightly watch and many a familiar faded dream.

       *   *   *   *

Below the boys' bedroom, Scarlet stares longingly out her kitchen window at the sunset whose scattered rays now resemble footlights bordering a rocky stage. Her thoughts are of the ongoing excitement of the theatre. How thrilling it once had been; how more so it must be now. But oh, how thrilling it once had been....

A brilliant orchestra tunes its handsome grained and golden instruments while backstage chorus members stretch tendons. Others warm their marvelously trained voices. It is opening night, December 3, 1953, pre-performance jitters nearly overcome young Scarlet. Although picked as a minor, obscure member of the large chorus, the show is the first musical version of the play 'Kismet'. Scarlet will proclaim proudly and forever how she was among this original Broadway cast.

Wrinkled in her nervous hands is a playbill with her very own stage name beneath a distinguished list of stars, all of whom she is honored this night to share the stage with: Alfred Drake, Doretta Morrow, Richard Kiley, Joan Diener and Henry Calvin.

Quivering helplessly, Scarlet peeks out from behind a huge dark velour curtain at the ever-growing audience. Shivering, she fights to hold still to absorb every impression. Like a frail animal sensing danger, she listens to the avalanche of bold talk that melts into whispers, whispers, a few stupid coughs followed by a prolonged suspenseful hush …………………….. Frightfully, a booming overture shatters all!

Shocked out of her reverie, Scarlet turns to rush to her place but stiffens. Before her waits the mighty and terrifying Wazir. Turning to escape, she now faces the young Caliph. Once more she turns and there before her stands the suavely bearded Hajj, romantic, poetic beggar (Alfie Drake) who was Chaplin, Coleman, Skinner,

Fairbanks and Nelson Eddy and more embodied into a single personality. This giant of the stage and screen is lost in concentration as he methodically prepares his entire being to power his ever-masterful magnificent entrance. He is quite unaware of the immature young lady who stares admiringly up at him.

Young Scarlet needed little excuse to fall in love. Her ambitious heart rushed in and out of love easily and often. But too often, the love she conceived was nourished and enlarged silently all within herself eventually to die and lie unburied like an unborn fetus that entombs its mother with it.

Yet here before her was a demigod who Athena patronized, Venus adored, and who theatre goers everywhere revered. Scarlet fantasized becoming his co-star in an Arabian Nights affair similar to the story in the show.

Abruptly, Scarlet is chased away by a production assistant. Confused by a thousand and one emotions, she dashes mindlessly past technicians and backstage activity into a colorfully crowded dressing room.

Nancy: Wake up, Scarlet! We're on. Wait. Where's your silk scarf? Never mind. Come on. Run! No, FLY!

Under offensive, blinding lights, before the entire world, out-of-tune, off-beat, clip-clop, screech-screech.

Nancy: Psst. Scarlet, now I know how it feels to be a tight-throated, horse's ass.

16

From the audience's perspective, the performers all appear to be thoroughly enjoying themselves, seemingly secure, even self-indulgent in their exotic roles. Close up, Scarlet is sweating profusely; self-torture is revealed in her revolving expressions. Eventually, her reprieve arrives with the grand finale's reprise:

Music in: "Night of My Nights"

(Reprise sung by the entire cast)

Play on the cymbal, a timbrel, a lyre.

Play with appropriate passion, fashion

Songs of delight and delicious desire,

For the night of my nights!

Somewhere enchanted my lover is waiting-

Where the rose and the jasmine ….. linger

While I tell her the moon is for mating,

And 'tis sin to be sing-gle!

Let peacocks and monkeys in purple adornings

Show her the way to my bridal ….. chamber.

Then get you gone till the morn of my mornings

After the night of my nights!

From the orchestra pit came a climatic crescendo. From heavenly balconies, merciful applause. Behind the curtain, smiles, aimless rushing about, cherishing embraces, kisses galore. From out of the blue, a gathering of blossoms is pressed into Scarlet's arms, with an accompanying note from...

Scarlet: A gentlemen admirer? Does anyone here know him?

Nancy: Looks like one of those big show-backing angels from out West.

Barrb: Hicksville, Idaho, M'am. B.W. Smenelli's the name.

Nancy: Oh, señor Spinelli, the producer!

Barrb: Heck, no, Miss. Friends just call me Barrb-Wire. (Smiling, looking about) Never been to any of these big stage shows before. Hardly figured seeing anything could jump out at 'cha and strike lightning like that. Didn't understand a bit of it, though. (Noticing their let down) But you were sure all mightily entertaining.

Disappointed by the cowboy's tactless wit and unimportance, Scarlet's fellow performers leave.

Scarlet: You needn't sulk, Mr. Smenelli. It wasn't anything you said. Speaking for all, thanks for your moral support. Now I really must go to my... (sings) "bridal chamber" ... where I'm sure a horrid little note – my nightly critique – clings to my makeup mirror. I performed quite abominably you know.

Barrb: Shucks, you sure were. Could hardly keep my peepers off ya. (Politely removes his western hat) I ah'd sincerely be honored if you'd join me for a right proper dinner date, Miss Scarlet.

Scarlet: If ever, Mr. Smenelli, it certainly shan't be this "the night of my nights". Our great guardian angel is throwing a fabulous and historical opening night publicity reception to be followed by a very private *soirée*. Every respectable heavenly body and star gazing columnist shall attend. *Zay gezunt.*

Barrb: What was that there you say?

Scarlet: Good-bye, Cowboy.

Scarlet never completed the long, successful run of the show. Soon after the opening, she was replaced and then resumed making those tedious rounds to find work. It was during these hard times when she finally consented to a "right proper dinner date".

Scarlet: (Amazed) 94 years old and still punches, did you say, 'buffalo'?

Barrb: On everyday but the Sabbath. Ole Granddad's been helping Pa work our little spread since I went off to vacation here. I don't expect to stay away much longer. I 'bout spent the last of my savings. (Pause) You crying, Miss Scarlet?

Scarlet: (Applying a tissue to her eyes) So then... you'll soon be saying *au revoir* to Manhattan's fanciest dining... and to me. (Smiling as she offers her hand across the table) I'll always remember these "right proper dinner dates" and the pleasant company of a genuine western gentleman. *Adieu, mon Cheri.*

Barrb: (Hesitantly taking her hand) I kinda been thinking. You suppose that a bright, honey-faced, show gal like yourself might consider marrying up to a dumb, ornery cuss like I be?

Scarlet: (Bitterly retracting her hand) It never fails.

Barrb: What do?

Scarlet: This uncomfortably trite scene I'm forced to play with you big spenders. Goodbye, Charlie.

Barrb: (Grabbing her wrist tightly) You weren't really being square with me, M'am, were ya? All that fool flitten, flirting, dry tears and dumb talk. I really ain't meant nothing to ya, did I?

Scarlet: Let go, Buster, or I'll call a cop. (Barrb releases her) Oh, you're so boringly naïve, Mr. B. W. Smenelli from Hicksville, Someplace.

Barrb: I made you an honest proposal, Miss Scarlet Something. I'd appreciate an honest answer, whatever it be.

Scarlet: (Impatiently gathering purse and gloves) Would a straight forward "NO" be sufficient without an explanation? Look, even if we were to somehow ignore the strong differences in our personalities, attitudes and familiar lifestyles, the biggest barrier to your unappreciated offer will always be my *yiddishe momme*.

Confused, Barrb closes one eye while wrinkling the other brow.

Scarlet: (Sitting) I'll put it this way—there was once a Yiddish gal who at the tender age of twenty-three dared to escape the watchful eyes of her darling Jewish mama. Later in Sheridan Square, the Village, she met a strong, virile irresistible *goyan*. Now one does not serve trayfer at an Orthodox Jewish table, nor does one *khosene hobn shiksers und goys*.

Barrb: (Embarrassingly) Girl boys?

Scarlet: (Smiles, shaking her head) Nor do I mean this Spanish painter, the state in central Brazil, nor goyel, a savior – which would have been great, but Oy! He was merely a *hofenunze groys gezunt goy* – a big, healthy, hopeless, non-Jewish boy. So she called to tell mama the shocking news. "Dear Mama", she cried, "I'm getting married". "A Jewish boy"?, "No, Mama". "A darlin' Jewish gell"? (pause) Mary Ann Balen, that's me. Mama's darlin' liddle Jewish gell. But since leaving home I've joined an artistic community where the strict moralities of Judaism are an invasion of privacy. My roommates at Bennington are into complete freedom of expression.

                  Hinduism, Zen and the occults are more tolerant to their indulging into astrology, drugs, unnatural sex practices, and even suicide. And as revolutionaries, teachers, artists, writers and performers, we are able to influence and alter society to comfort ourselves.

Barrb: Boy, that's a lot to make the devil real proud.

Scarlet: The devil and God don't exist. In nature everything's the same.

Barrb:	(Standing, drops a one thousand dollar bill on the table) By the way, if everythang be the same, there ain't no good or evil.
Scarlet:	Exactly. These vary with different cultures from time to time.
Barrb:	And everythang being the same, the seeds and offspring of David ain't any better'n fertilized weeds. S'long, M'am.
Scarlet:	(Jumping up explosively) No! No! Jews are not weeds! Did weeds follow the golden path of prophecy? Prophecy being fulfilled to this day and I can prove it by comparing Hebrew scripture with history. Can you deny my Jewish ancestry has remained strong and united through all the persecution while our countless godless enemies were continually defeated and destroyed?
Barrb:	Yeah, whenever the Israelites fell from the Lord.
Scarlet:	We made mistakes. Hasn't every nation taken other paths, at times, away from God? But we've returned. So, bravo Israel, home at last!
Barrb:	Yeah, more than once. Funny, you sure don't sound like any 'a them educated friends you talked about.

Scarlet: Mr. Smenelli, my heart may be aroused by erotic passions of Ancient Greece, the wantonness of pagan rites, but through this self-same heart courses burning Jewish blood. (drops onto her chair) Though you couldn't understand.

Barrb: (Returns to her) I understand rightly, Miss Scarlet. Kinda' feel the same 'bout the sweet, comforting faith of my own folks. Yeah, I'm sometimes unruly, work till I drop for what a dollar can get me. Yet deep inside (meets her sincerely eye to eye) I believe you and I both feel the same 'bout what the all-important thing in our lives must be. (hat on) *Adiós* and keep the change. (exits)

Waiter: Pardon, Mademoiselle Roussir. We'll be closing soon. (In French) How was your wine?

      *   *   *   *

Within a few years, Scarlet finally gave up the uncertainty of the stage and the artists' colony for lifelong companionship with a steadfast cowpoke from Hicksville, Someplace.

She sadly recalled that final evening before she, her mulatto infant and Barrb drove far off from Broadway. In those final moments, she and Nancy exchanged tearful goodbyes outside their beloved forum for creative expression, the theatre. They gave a true performer's parting, everything phrased with clear facial expressions.

As Scarlet and Barrb drove away, a magnitude of bright lights melted into night's obscure haze.

*   *   *   *

Now years later in her kitchen, Scarlet's emotions burst forth hopelessly in uncontrolled breaths. Tears destroying visions of that time long ago and far away, she reminisces over a large steaming pot of Idaho stew.

*   *   *   *

In the darkened stable, face half-hidden in shadow, Barrb sponges down his Arabian quarter gelding Wildfire.

Barrb: I just know she's angry 'nough to warm that ole' stew pot. Knows darn well I hate yesterday's stew heated up again. Steady, Wildfire. Whoa. Stand your ground. Wait'll the boys are more grown, they'll forget all this-here show biz foolishness. And by next harvest, with all the work and just rewards, all our kin and good folk getting together celebrating, all will surely be forgotten. Steady now boy.

Barrb towel dries Wildfire and throws a blanket across his back. After a fond pat, Barrb carries the saddle outside and rests it on the corral fence. Wearing a tired smile, he pauses to reflect upon the last of the sunset. In ghostly form, his sons appear as in earlier years. Happily, they rush up and hug their dad endearingly. It was the remembrance of a time of unhesitant, unabashed closeness, when his family was loving and eternal.

Barrb: Tony-Boy, Joe-B. Look at them colors in that-there striped sky. Who needs a fancy paint'n, huh? Seems our Lord's trying to tell us something. Bet if we were patient and stood here long enough, we'd see the answer to everything written right across the glorious sky. Here's something else betcha never thought about.

   Kneeling, takes a handful of soil.

Barrb: Dirt. Plain ole' dirt. Plain ole' sun, air. (looking up and shaking the dirt in his fist) It's all some wonderful magic how one day your pa went along and lucked out on a mightly good woman. Two became one. Then wonder of wonders, come yau precious children. Scientists ain't never described the great powers of our mysterious Creator that way. It's best to keep things simple. That's all there is to it. All you, me or anyone ever needs. Someday you little pups'll grow up to realize....

   His sons suddenly, simultaneously turn their heads toward a golden path that has lit mysteriously. Drawn by the music and something glowing in the distance, the boys run off down the illuminated path, laughing. They vanish over the hill and their lighted way disappears.

Barrb: Boys! Come back here! I said come
                back! You won't find anything greater
                on down Lucifer's trail to temptation!
                It's all right 'chere! Lord, I-I'm trying...
                but I-I can't seem to...."

Weakly, Barrb falls to his knees and hopelessly bows
his head. His fists pressed tightly to his stomach against
the pain of having lost something precious then whimpers.

Barrb: It's sacred I tell ya. Your grand-pa
                and great-grannie folk... the bones,
                dreams and spirits of our right beloved
                kin's what make it sacred. (Pause) I
                must sound like some ignorant ole'
                injun praying to his ancestors. (Facing
                skywards) Dear Lord, I know you
                cares about my boys. They being
                your children 'fore they's ever mine.
                You know I fear letting them go their
                own way, way things be out there.
                But if 'n you're sending them into the
                land of idol worshippers like you did
                them there prodigal son, or to open
                their eyes by blindness and suffrage
                like Samson amongst them-there
                Philistines, I know you've written a
                right proper ending to their life story
                and by Thy will, so be it, Amen.

The sun has dropped behind the ridge. As we back
away, Barrb resembles a stern blackened sculpture
shrinking against the dying glow on the horizon.

*   *   *   *

SCENE: Many years later, upon a highland meadow commanding an exceptional view of the majestic mountains surrounding the Smenelli Ranch. This location, camera angle and music suggest the opening scene from Sound of Music.

Tony, now a mature man, runs across the meadow ala' Julie Andrews. The music stops. Arms upheld, Tony appears to belt out a song. But his voice is barely audible. Mangy (son of Scamp) tugs on Tony's pants cuff.

Tony: (Trying to shake the dog loose) Git! Git! Swear I'll kick you, Mangy. Alright, here's a Snark Bar. Now shhash! Go! Git! (Mangy snaps candy and runs off) Darn. Can't figure how Hollywood does some things. Bet they taped Miss Andrews singing in some fancy studio. Cause when the wind breathes in the wrong direction, the acoustics up here's really lousy. Hey, Joe-B! You hear me singing from over there?!!

Joe: Save your tonsils, Tony-Boy! They ain't never gonna hear you in New York!!

Tony: (Running to Joe agitated) Ain't nobody trying to be heard all the way to New York, you darn fool! (Arriving out of breath) Ma said... Rich Burton... got himself a mighty powerful voice... by trying to outshout the Welsh Ocean's roar.

Joe: That ain't nothing. Pa said Marl Brando prefected his voice by out-wesp'ring a wee, drunk mouse (imitating Brando) while he spied a bitty fly flitten 'round the room. (Grudgingly snatching up a hay bale) Heck, what good's all our smarts doing us? We'll never be nothing but sweaty, stinking cowpoke. Come on. Let's get 'er done. And put your teeny hat on fore you bake your brains.

Tony: (Picking up his hat) Ain't teeny at all. Sets just the right image for a handsome cowboy hero type like I be (putting it on carefully). That thang you got on's so ugly, bet it's that same stupid thang Bob Hope throwed away after making them funny westerners.

Joe: (Walter Brennen) It's a gen-u-ine pony express rider hat worn by Uncle Jess Edwards (Cary Grant) and you know that. Might'n be much on looks but sure keeps off the hot sun while keeping in precious body heat.

Tony: (Tipping up Joe's hat) I think you're getting too much a' that precious heat. Your hair's starting to frizzle.

Joe: You're just jealous 'cause you don't share my royal Africana bloodline, Honky.

Tony: You can joke about some calling you part negro, but it 'fenda me terrible. The fact they won't believe we brothers come from our same Ma and Pa, and like Pa already proved, you inherited a lot more than I on Pa's Grandma Lezwak which 'splains' you being a bit darker and so on than I am.

Joe: Yeppin, that's the God's honest truth and can't be denied. For under it all, we're exactly the same. Except for t'way how our different brains are set up and operate, maybe. (They hug)

Tony: But we're still brothers which is all I cares about.

Joe: I don't want no sisters. Whatever her color or what her hair looked like, the rest would really make us different and difficult to identify with.

Tony: Hey, 'nough of that serious talk — you know what? These hats need are 'scape valves.

Joe's face lights up with an idea. They gesture back and forth.

Joe: Am I thinking what you're thinking?

Tony: That neat hat trick we figured up for
                   a movie?

Joe: Let's practice.

Like two hardened gunfighters, the brothers adjust their hats, holsters, spin their pistols, then stand nose to nose stern at the ready. Suddenly they snatch off one another's hats, toss these into the air and shoot repeatedly up at them. Now ventilated, their hats fall back atop their heads.

Tony: I still need inspiring (turns on portable
                   radio).

Joy: Hey! (examining his hat) You blew the
                   top right off! Made me a target for
                   every vulture in the district.

Well-tanned and muscular, the brothers smile, sing and dance to the music while moving hay bales with enormous energy, speed and power. Tony flips off the radio, leans exhausted against the hay and takes a letter from his pocket.

Joe: You reading the letter from that-there
                   New York agent again?

Tony: Suppertime, I'm showing this to Pa.

Joe: You ain't got the nerve.

Tony: Wanna bet?

Joe: This Jap radio and my boots 'gainst your ole rodeo buckle.

Tony: My feet'd have to grow twice their size to fill them buckets. And if I were king of the world, last thing I'd part with is this one of a kind, grand prize rodeo buckle.

Joe: Which you chiseled from me for two dollars and a Yoo-Hoo.

Tony: Now no one wants ta' hear 'bout ancient history. How much ya got to lose?

Joe: Hey. You're talking to big money here. Just dip into your jeans down to your socks, Brother. I'll match anything you come up with.

Kneeling on the grass, they hurriedly lay out their few coins, pocket knives, pine nuts, candy, etc.

Joe: Okay, that-there's sixty-seven cents....

Tony: Hold on Joe-B. What the heck we doing? (Pocketing his possessions) This got nothing to do with us growing old and a wasting away here in Hicksville... (holds up letter) when New York is begging for our talents.

Joe:	You're the one with all the talent. I'm just a bit of background accompliment. So for me to be, or for not to be.... one of them big show stars? I kinda dropped that inclination at a horse stop somewhere back on the trail. Getting too old, I guess.
Tony:	You ain't ever too old in show biz, Joe-B. Lookie there at Ed Asner on TV.
Joe:	Loonie Tunes, Brother 'fore you's born to boots, Ma played on stage with Ed in the "Three Cent Op'ry". So lookie how long it took 'em to make it. And he's good.
Tony:	You sure got more excuses to stay in your goose down feather bed.
Joe:	Besides I been 'sidering posing serious marriage to my sweet little bird-singing Katie.
Tony:	You ain't ever gonna marry Katie and you know it.
Joe:	When I consider how that poor Umpqua gal's been tolerating me and my plutonic courtship all these years. Yep. Mind's made up. So don't try'n stop us or'n the Love Bug what's be giving us the itches in our britches.

Tony: You think I'd try? What's the use? Be like trying to stop a bellyful of belches. It'd only erupt some other time and place.

Joe: Just like Ma. Using kindly agreeable words to trick me into something I don't want to do.

Tony: No, go on. Harness up to that poor innocent thing and rot here in Hicksville. In the news, you read about terrible things like that everyday. You've surely forgotten them mightly aspiring words we swore to.

Joe: How could I? Reciting 'em every night after choir practice... which I can't see got a thing to do with marrying Katie.

Tony: No, you wouldn't see. You wouldn't one teeny bit. Joe-B, we've been brothers my whole life.

Joe: So?

Tony: Does anything have to make sense between us? Has it ever?

Joe: Well ...

Tony: If not for me, say it for the old Gipper?

Joe: Well ...

Tony: For the Duke? (pause) The King?

Joe:	The King. You talking 'bout Cole, Elvis, Roy or Clark?
Tony:	All the Kings … their horses, too.
Joe:	Wow. Okay. Stand back! Here goes. "As God is my wintness… as God is my wintness… I'm going to live thru this here and when it's over…!"
Tony:	(Overlapping) Joe-B. Joe-B. Take five. Cut! Only the devil points his fists at Heaven. Besides, them ain't the mightly aspiring words I meant.
Joe:	Well, just which mightly aspiring ones we talking about now.
Tony:	(Singing) "Surely as I was born and 'll someday die…", recollect now?
Joe:	(Nods) "And as surely as God created all things for a reason…." You sure that includes you and me too, Tony-Boy?
Tony:	"We Smenelli brothers surely weren't born just to snooze in the sun, watch football and chase…"
Joe:	"Down the road after ice cream and pizza trucks. No, siree, Bob. This here entire whole world's sorta like a…"
Tony:	All the world's a stage, Joe-B.
Joe:	Yep and we're all just stage hands.

Tony:	(Looking at the sun) Spotlight's ever shining on every single soul.
Joe:	But bitty time to do what we gotta.
Tony:	And it don't mean milking goats or mucking out barns.
Joe:	Suppose I'll just get married and ...
Tony:	You're too old, Joe-B. But ...
Both:	... you ain't ne'ary too old in show biz.
Joe:	Oh, heck. We ain't never done a two-step out of Hicksville, or ever gonna.
Tony:	We sure have, Joe-B. Every time we dreamed what'd be like to be star entertainers. Getting invited to all them fancy parties. Meeting big celebrities. Our pictures and names writ up in magazines (hand Joe letter). Better read'er again for encouragement.
Joe:	Hard to believe. A genuine invite from a hi-class, New York agent. (Hands back letter) It still ain't no bonafide, lawyer made up certified and autographed contract.
Tony:	Know your problem, Joe-B? No vision, no faith, no bank account, no future, no deodorant, no nothing.

Joe: You 'spect me to hand over fifty dollars or more gas money, give up my home, Ma's on time meals and go with you just on blind faith?

Tony: (Hands on Joe's shoulders) Home cooking, you just stay here and rot in your ole smelly boots. (Shoves Joe as he moves away)

Joe: That's it. Lights! Camera! Action! Smash! (Knocking Tony hard to the ground)

Tony: (Sitting up stunned) See what this wild country's done to you, Joe-B? Instead of a brilliant star of stage and screen, you've become a grizzly barbarian like Billy the Kid, Jesse James, Hoover Garrison the dog-catcher and all the rest. You need sincere prayer and patience, boy.

Joe: (Stamping about mocking) Listen who's parlor talking 'bout patience. (Hat off) There he be, Lord! The world's greatest sinner. (On his knees) Don't let him wrangle free this time. Go on. Send on down a lightning bolt that'll ...

Tony: (Pushes Joe off balance) Yap-up, you darn fool. Now listen. Last night a pretty angel came to me.

Joe: Not again.

Tony:	"Get off your wallet and skedaddle", she said. Joe-B, I'm finally leaving Ma and Pa, them dumb cows and you for good.
Joe:	(Rises. They brush dirt off each other.) Minds all saddled up, huh?
Tony:	Yep.
Joe:	Whelp, (meaningless sniff) don't forget to pay your store bill. (Walks to wagon)
Tony:	Store bill?!
Joe:	You ain't sticking me with your I.O.U.'s.
Tony:	That's all you're concerned with? Well this's mighty surprising coming from my own life long brother. Well, so long, stranger. Since you ain't fixing on joining me on my world tour, well-ll that's just ...
Joe:	(Calmly) I'm going.
Tony:	... fine with ... You are? Why?
Joe:	Try and recollect your happy 7th birthday, T.B. We sat down there'n our ole rotted stump. Being your elder brother, I swore I'd never leave ya.
Tony:	I'd sure like to remember that. You sure it weren't no dream or from some movie we saw?

Joe: Sometimes it's just too hard to tell. Every moment that goes past ends up behind me kinda like I dreamed it. Soon everything, even the things people tell me and what I make up all mixes together like batter. But somewhere out here or in my heart I made you a promise. So (sniffs) guess it means I'm going.

Tony: (With open arms) ahh, yip-pee-ki-yon-away! Oh, Pancho!

Joe: Oh, Cisco! (Embracing)

Tony: You should be an actor, Joe-B. Cause you sure had me fooled.

Joe: No. I meant it.

Tony: In my opinion, you're as fine an actor as they be. (Joe smiles shyly) Now Pa'll have to hire on more'n fifty hands to do all our chores.

Joe: First thing he'll do is throw a mighty, Mangy fit.

Mangy's ears perk at the sound of his name.

Tony: Won't have to tell him, J-B. I'll just show him this here letter from my agent. A letter's worth a thousand words.

39

Joe: Lookie yonder. There's ole Pa now, sod busting, hooting and hollering like all get out. Must be heading for a gold strike, the out-house or home cooking.

Tony: Can't be lunch time. We'd heard the clanger get beat up.

Joe: 'Cording to the sun 'tis. And there's Ma on the back porch 'bout to whoop'er now.

Tony: Joe-B. Ever wonder what dumb movie Ma got that idea from? (Down on the back porch Scarlet beats the dinner triangle) Heck! We're forgetting what's waiting for whoever's the last one in.

Joe: Won't be me. Hop in the wagon and hang on fierce. I'm taking the reins.

Tony: (Remains composed on the ground as Joe scurries onto the wagon seat) Boy, now you're gonna see some fancy mule-skinning. (Whipping the reins) Hiy-yah! Hiy-yah!

The horse strains and rears, but is unable to budge the wagon. Bewildered, Joe looks around.

Joe: You holding this thing back?

Tony: Sure, I'm the Super Cosmic Cowboy. Ease'er on back a bit.

After removing the wheel blocks, Tony leaps into the driver's seat, tumbling Joe backwards into the wagon bed. Tony recovers the reins, releases the handbrake and heads down the rugged slope trying desperately to catch Barrb who is far ahead on horseback.

Joe: Watch out for them big ruts coming up!

After a series of serious high bouncing, Joe leans close again to Tony's ear.

Joe: Go back!

Tony: What!

Joe: Said turn around and go back! I think you might have missed one of them big, nasty bumps back there.

Tony: We must be plumb loco chasing down the side of a cliff. If this rig flips, we're dead.

Joe: Betcha the best stuntmen in Hollywood wouldn't do this for less'n (spreads fingers) five bucks.

As Tony fights the reins, trying to control the bouncing wagon, Joe lightens the load by tossing hay bales overboard. Some bounce out unassisted.

Tony: What you doing? The lighter we get the more we might flip!

Joe: Well, I seen this done in a nifty airplane flick. Big John lost all his engines 'cept one which was spitting fire and burning up the wing!

Tony: Joe-B! You got that movie all mixed, mashed and mutilated. It was a sinking remake of "Life Boat". And to lighten the load, that actor who played the best Zorro ever threw that fellow from the "Life of Riley" overboard to sharks. Then he sacrificed Lloyd Nolan of loose denture fame. Both were Zorro's best friends, but to save the others... Ah, both were sick and dead anyway.

Joe: You sure that's the one I meant?

Tony: Yep. Cause if you seen it, so did I.

Joe: Then how come I (looks ahead, eyes widen) d-yi-yi!!

The wagon crashes thunderously into the goat shed. Barrb and Scarlet rush into the shed and find their boys safe among the animals and hay.

*   *   *   *

Stripped to his long underwear, Barrb seated in the water trough, chuckles while splashing his sons and their dog. Wearing only boots, colorful shorts with Afro designs and an Indian head dress, Joe scrubs his father's back while Tony, in hat and pajama bottoms, mans the hand pump.

Barrb: Guess you boys won't be doing much betting 'gainst me for a while. Losing to one's own pappy can be pretty embarrassing. Just suppose some sweet, young gal were to drive up here right now?

(Having earlier sighted) A Ranchero pickup drives to the back porch. Its door marked: "Mist O'Morn Nursery, Hicksville, Idaho". The delicate driver, shocked by the sight of her three nearly naked neighbors, remains holding her wheel tightly, eyes fixed ahead. Joe remains by the water trough while his father and brother creep curiously to the pickup and study the frozen face of the driver. After a moment, the driver's eyes shift to her two hairy and sudsy observers. Fighting her outrage, she relaxes her grip on the wheel, looks to her mirror and hums as she casually combs her long, Indian raven black hair. Then, taking a deep breath and clearing her throat, with a pert smile and composure, she finally steps from the pickup.

Shy and emotional, Kathleen (Katie) Sequaya O'Neal is well mannered, home spun and personable. Though in her mid-thirties she appears much younger. Her voice is an added embellishment to her delightful personality and appearance. It is a cultured, well-tuned instrument which all might have enjoyed. But other than privately and in church choir she and her gifted attributes are destined to become among the many uncelebrated treasures cast into oblivion.

Katie: Good afternoon, Mr. Smenelli.

Barrb:	Well, afternoon to ya, my pretty Miss Katie. How's your lovely little Ma and that chiseling ole Pa of yours?
Katie:	Oh, they're real fine, Sir. How's Mrs. Smenelli?
Barrb:	Scarlet's just fine, real fine, couldn't be much finer.
Katie:	Oh, that's fine. Afternoon, Joseph. (No reply) Je regrette. Afternoon, Antonio.

Barrb returns to the trough for his back scrub.

Tony:	Noon to you, Katie. I'm fine. Let me fetch those empty cans off your tail end.

Tony goes to the back of her small pickup and lifts out stainless steel containers which he sets on the porch.

Katie:	*Merci*, gallant Antoine. Joe?
Barrb:	(Over his shoulder) Harder! (Joe scrubs harder) Owhh!

The kitchen door squeaks open. Scarlet, carrying a cream canister of milk makes a pretentious theatrical entrance onto the back porch.

Scarlet:	My! But isn't this a glorious day to be alive in Hicksville? (Shocked) Joe-B! Stop that! And fetch your clothes. Your father's big enough to scrub his own back! My! My goodness, Kathleen. Aren't men embarrassing? I must apologize.
Katie:	It's alright, Mrs. Smenelli. I'm kinda used to it by now.
Scarlet:	Oh bless you, my dear, for always saying the right things. Kindly stay for lunch. I've prepared a fine southern cuisine. The recipe's been in my Georgian family for ages.
Barrb:	No boiled chicken and matzo crackers again.
Scarlet:	...which only a fine lady would appreciate.
Katie:	No thank you, M'am. But there is a serious matter I wish to discuss with Hosiah. Joe?
Barrb:	He's hiding 'hind the wagon trying to get his britches over them big buckets of his. What's the trouble, gal? Want him to saw off his engagement ring? I'll bet it's 'bout shrunk tight around your finger. Should be after twelve years.
Scarlet:	Shush up. That's no concern of yours.

Barrb: If that boy entered more rodeos and less movie houses he'd be a high standing stud sporting us sprite little grandchildren by now. The fact he ain't, concerns me strongly.

Scarlet: (Smiling at Katie) Here's this mornings milk, dear. I believe it requires one more filtering. Again, I must apologize for the men. They've highly upset the poor goats. I fear they won't milk more'n a squirt or two by evening.

Katie: Oh, this will be fine, M'am. Most of the orphaned colts at the nursery are on regular formula now. And Mother and I aren't expecting any new babies (staring sadly at Joe) not for a while anyhow.

Joe: (Still tripping over his half-on pants, notices everyone's eyes on him) Forget it, folks, I'm not up to what you're all thinking.

Barrb: Then I guess we can trust you to accompany Sweet Little Katie Bluegown home without need of a chaperone to slap down your paws.

Joe: (Tripping half dressed as he helps Katie into her pickup) If you don't mind, I'll finish dressing behind your truck.

Katie: No, dear. I don't mind.

Joe: There're some things I won't be able
                  to do here to please some folks 'cause
                  there is some things that me and Tony...

Tony: ... will tell you all about it after supper.
                  Get going, Joe-B. And you better tell
                  Katie what we decided. (Joe replies
                  with a wink and hand signal.)

Katie and Joe drive off.

Barrb: (Looking after) I'm sure he loves that
                  sweet gal. Wonder what's holding him
                  back?

              *   *   *   *

Katie and Joe riding along in her pickup.

Joe: (Sniffing) You got on some kinda
                  perfume?

Katie: Jest a smutch!

Joe: There's more'n a smutch in the breeze
                  and it sure ain't me.

Katie: I know.

Joe: You suggesting I smell bad?

Katie: Yes.

Joe: Work-like or body wise?

Katie:	Both! Breath wise too! What did you eat?
Joe:	Nothing since breakfast.
Katie:	Which was?
Joe:	Just some smoked trout snatched from the bone and spread on a garlic loaf.
Katie:	A "fishmush" sandwich! And you knew we'd be riding together this afternoon. Joe-B, time's a passing. We just got to talk marriage. I'm growing old.
Joe:	How old?
Katie:	None of your business.
Joe:	I know it anyhow.
Katie:	You sure are romantic.
Joe:	Why should I be? We're not married. Want I should get us both worked up and sicker'ner'na castrated hog. (Silence. Joe humming a song.) Case you've forgotten, that used to be our song.
Katie:	It still is our song to me, Joe-B. And I want you should know: I really don't need no kissing, no hugging, no... no nothing. Just your love and devotion... and having you near. (She begins humming then sings "The Nearness of You".)

Don't need no pale moon to excite me, to warm and delight me. Oh no, it's just the nearness of you.

Joe: When you're in my arms and I feel you so close to me all my wildest dreams come true.

Katie: Don't need no soft lights to enchant me, if you'll only grant me the right to hold your memory so tight and to feel in the night the nearness of you.

Joe: And I want you to know, Katie, no matter how far 'way I be, you'll always be this near to me. Cause I'll always love you.

Katie: As will I, Joe-B, as will I.

* * * *

That evening, Scarlet serves chicken, biscuits and buttered corn with hammy elegance. After prayers, the men bless themselves then attack the chow, scooping up huge servings.

At supper's end, Scarlet returns from the kitchen with a tray full of hot apple turnovers. Like a tipsy clown on a bucking bronco she stumbles to the table yelling "Get that dumb goat out of my way"! The boys intercept her tray as Barrb grabs and whirls her about. (Bursts of laughter follow.)

Barrb:	Wasn't they were drunk, Scarlet. You saw them out front pulling, 'lowing their dumb horse up on the buckboard to ride a spell. I'll bet that ole mare couldn't steer them two mules worth a lick. (Laughter)
Tony:	Hey Mom. Show us some fancy stage stepping.
Barrb:	How 'bout you boys striking up the band while your Ma and I demonstrate some real down hom' Tennessee mule footing. Pardon me, My Light O' Love. Might I have the honor.
Scarlet:	Not quite sure, Mr. Smenelli from Hicksville, Someplace. We hardly know one another. (Teeth closed) Is this the step ole Uncle Jess Edwards showed us?
Tony:	(While tuning his guitar, aside to Joe) It's true. They still don't know each other.
Joe:	(Tuning his fiddle) They're doing just fine. Come on, folks. Pick up your heels and stomp.
Scarlet:	Hit it, Boys! Whee!
Barrb:	(Dancing as he sings)
	Standing on the porch with roses in my hand.

Give it to ya, Honey, if ya let me be your man.

Come out tonight. Please come out tonight.

Oh, hey Honey, won't you come out tonight.

Here comes pretty lady all dressed in blue.

Say hey, Honey, couldn't want no one but you.

Tony: He's in a mightly receptive mood, Joe-B. Good time to spring this letter on him.

Joe: Don't trust a wild cat. Even when he's kitteny playful.

Barrb yelps as he leaps over the table chasing Scarlet.

Scarlet: (Singing as she dances, twirling swiftly away) Who's that a honking, coming cross my field, jumping and a bumping... (Exhibiting dizziness, Scarlet stops and is helped to her chair).

Oh, my, my, my. These legs belong to a much, much older woman. Tony, reach me my pillow and my quilt, please, dear.

Barrb:	(Removing her shoes) Shouldn't try so hard to impress everyone, Scarlet.
Scarlet:	(Pulling her feet away) I wasn't trying to impress anyone. These are my children. (Sore) Ohhh.
Tony:	(Kneeling to rub her feet) Feet hurt, Ma?
Joe:	(Pats Tony's shoulder) You sure were doing some fancy tripping there, Ma.
Scarlet:	(Smiling up, finger to chin) The Virginia reel or that old buck and wing I did in Showboat?
Joe:	(Lost for words) Wow. Was so fast, I'm not sure.
Scarlet:	You know I despise braggarts, but I once performed ... (Her sons joining in) twenty consecutive back flips down the center aisle after an all-night rehearsal. (Barrb motions a warning and the boys quit mocking.) Then I went on to perform impeccably in two matinees plus an evening performance. (Head laid back limply) And, then we partied all that night toasting Bacchus and the Muses.
Barrb:	Choose ye this day whom ye will serve.

Scarlet: (Flourishing her hands like a sorcerer. Her dark gaze intent on recreating lost visions.) At the hofbrau I drank and sang with the royal Student Prince. Lost a most passionate poetic duel to the most virile, rugged Stosh Kowalski ever. With mystic Oberon I danced thru weed, willow and fire, flew deeper and deeper into an enchanted briary wood.

Barrb: Do all to the glory of God.

Scarlet: Oh, those titillating contacts with fascinating celebrities. Uhn, Le theatre de la foire. Ah, la musica comedie-en-vaudivilles. How many memorable performances have I missed since settling way out here in the boonies with your Pa? "La boonies" (Chuckles) isn't that a ridiculous location for a bright and shiny star?

Barrb: Yep, sure is something the way our Lord put stars to shining, even way out'ch here even in the boondocks lighting the way to Heaven for them what aren't so glued to this world – this fool's dream.

Tony: (Singing from "Godspell", 'mockingly) Pre-e-e-pare ye the way of the Lord!

Barrb: Is this all there is? Or is there eternal bliss? (Tony repeats)

Scarlet:	Stop it! Stop it! (Lowers her head)
Barrb:	Now, Scarlet, we mustn't get upset over nothing.
Scarlet:	(Shaking off his touch, snaps her head violently) Don't! (Smiling) No, Boys. Don't stop playing. Music is life. Music is life.
Tony:	What would y... you like to hear, Ma?
Scarlet:	Oh ... (Dreamily) a romantic serenade, por favor. No. Play some jazzy jive to jitterbug to. Something to set my head a spinning, my shimmy, shimmy skirt a-twirl. Play the tall trees to swaying. Tempestuous tunes I'm a-saying. Play for Indian rain. Coax down a joy of jumping jellybeans upon fields full of funny faces. Play us hops and jumps and fast running races. Play in a gay parade with flapping flags unfurled, big dance bands and a lover's charade. Play me them razzle dazzle days I danced as a girl.
Joe:	(Confused) Uh ...
Scarlet:	(Touching his hand) Never mind, dear. Just play some sweet reverie from any old musical. (Singing) I love you, Por-gy!
Joe:	(Singing) Bess, you is my wom-man ...

Scarlet: (Singing) B Flat, D, Joseph. B Flat, D. I love you Porgy.

Joe: (Singing on key now) Bess, you is my woman now!

Tony: (Seeing his mother's tears) Wouldn't you rather hear something brighter, Ma?

Joe: (Excited) How 'bout ... (playing and singing, Tony joining) "There's no business like show ..."

Barrb: Enough. Time we practiced for the Calgory Stampede.

Ignoring their protests, Barrb demonstrates his rodeo techniques using Joe as his quarter horse and Tony for a roping calf. Scarlet hobbles angrily across the room. Hooting and yelping, she beats a sarcastic silent movie accompaniment on the piano, beating herself to emotional exhaustion.

Meanwhile, her three weary wranglers kneel side by side on the floor. Barrb proudly embraces his sons' shoulders:

Barrb: It sure'd be a great day in the morn when all three a'us are featured together at the Great Roundup.

Joe: Guess I'm getting old, Pa. Don't care much for competing anymore. I just want to enjoy life.

Barrb:

Without competition there just can't be no life, son. Everybody, before they're even born, swam the great swim of life agin millions of competitors all fighting to stay alive and come into this world. But only one's got the superior power, energy and driving guts. Even after a life of struggle, not every survival will make that final flight upstream to spawn. Some will die childless without ever passing on their precious genes. But I'd say you boys are onery 'nough to chaw bear claws and leap Hanged Ear Canyon. Come on. Who's gonna win a big, silver buckle this season?

Looking to each other for a sign, the brothers rise and move away. Barrb's eyes following suspiciously.

Scarlet:

Show him that letter, son.

Tony:

(Taking the letter from his pocket) Here, Pa.

Barrb:

(Putting on his spectacles, reads the letter.) For a second there I thought it might be a greet'n from Uncle Sam's army. No, just some sly scheming New York talent agent (rips letter to shreds). Come look out the window. See it? It's all yours. This house, the land, them mountains, that blazing sky. Everything your heart cherishes is all yours. Boy, you sure got a pretty sunset.

Scarlet:	They've seen a thousand suns go down – each the same shade of macho blood and bruises bursting over another dying day.
Barrb:	I was addressing my sons.
Tony:	Then listen to us, Pa! We don't favor dying in your boots, don't want your legacy, land, chattel, none of it.
Joe:	Guess being a buckaroo ain't in our stars. So what ya say, Pa?
Barrb:	I... I... say... Oh Lord, what is your will?
Scarlet:	We want an answer now!
Barrb:	Would a straight honest NO do you? It's not what they, you or I want... but what the Lord wants. That's my answer.
Scarlet:	It's just too ridiculous – telling grown men what to do. Look at your sons, Barrb. They're fully grown men now.
Barrb:	You look, Scarlet. They're only growed on the outside. We've got their insides so confused, they don't know whether to get their horses shod or shuffle off to Buffalo.
Scarlet:	They're going.

Barrb: What for? Work? They got this ranch here. Friends? Ain't a family in ten miles they don't know personally. Good, clean minded folk who you can always count on. Nice little school, full goods general store, a solid bank, good Doc Dubin, fine full gospel church, an honest local government, a sheriff who offers home cooking and friendly sermons and jobs to his lockups. Even a darn good little movie house.

Scarlet: Dear little Hicksville. What a blessing of variety you offer.

Barrb: When I vacationed in the big city and met you, Scarlet, I walked through such crowds, never caught an eye. Hardly met the folks in the next hotel room. Young girls hanging on boys hanging on corners without a thing good to do. Young men and old spreading wild seeds carelessly in gutters. No telling who or what our boys'll meet up with there. Cons, crooks, pimps, peeps, cheats, liars, addicts, murderers maybe. Oh, what a variety of the devil's blessings are waiting our easy pickings, ignorant sons.

Scarlet: What can be more distorted than the picture you've presented? I've told them of the wonders they'll see: the opportunities, luxuries, excitement, those bright lights.

Barrb: Go on, Scarlet. Tell the rest. What's it like when all them lights go out? When you're out in the street, deserted by all your friends, cheated on? Fighting, cursing, clawing with your lover – that "most passionate poetic duel" as you put it. Boys, I once searched the city for someone I loved and nearly lost forever.

Scarlet: (Tormented to tears) Like all men, you couldn't love anyone but yourself.

Barrb: Finally found her in a dirty flop joint. I ask you now... what sort of creature would cut its veins then stick its head inside a gas oven, praying to die? Leaving to the world it hated a sickly child to hide itself in a dark corner –frightened and confused, poor lovely little thang and another precious, innocent one growing fatherless and blind inside her otherwise empty belly.

Scarlet: Shut up! Stop it! You're still jealous! But I won't reveal why – not before my own dear children! Mine! You hear? Not yours. Mine!

Barrb: Damn you, lady. (Slaps Scarlet)

Joe pushes his father away, about to strike him. Tony grabs Joe and both brothers fall backwards to the floor.

Barrb:	Looks like sentiment fell on your side again. Reckon I'll just let our boys go the hard road after all. (Eyes uplifted) So be it. (Staring intently at his sons) Tomorrow morn, I want both you boys out. (Barrb walks solemnly up to his room.)
Scarlet:	No, Barrb! They waited so long to prevent this. Come back; give them encouragement. They only wanted your blessing. Come back; let them go in peace! Don't let it be this way … Dear.

*   *   *   *

Early next morn, in the driveway beside the Smenelli ranch house. Scarlet and Katie watch as the brothers finish packing their '51 coupe convertible. Signs on its doors and trunk read: "Lookout Broadway! Here come the Smenelli bros"! Nearby Mangy frolics and chases Ms. Prim, Mr. Peabody and Ginger (elder goat and geese).

As the last of their belongings are loaded, Tony calls Mangy and the dog jumps happily aboard. Joe stares up at the closed curtains of the second-floor window.

Scarlet:	He's too bullheaded. He won't come down.
Joe:	I know, Ma.
Tony:	Come here, you pretty gals and give me and my pardner a big, Broadway goodbye kiss.

Scarlet: (Proudly fondling Tony's face) Since you were born, I charted your destiny in favorable stars. That winning smile. (Tony forms a funny face) Oh, get out of here – and go for it. (Final kiss)

Tony: You bet, M'am. (Jumps into driver's seat, starts car) Hey, Joe-B! Unbridle that pretty choir gal. These horses are breathing hot and heavy.

Joe: "Then wipe their sweat and don't give 'em drink 'till sundown".

Tony: (Pointing) Gable to Stu Erwin. "Chained", MGM, 1934.

Katie: If only we had more time, Joe-B. (Joe embraces and kisses her.)

Tony: Turn it off, Lover Boy! Saddle up here and let's ride.

Joe: S'long, Katie girl. Be back 'soon as Tony is hooked up with a big show.

Joe pulls away, yelps and takes a running jump into his seat. Mangy flops upon Joe's lap.

Katie: How long might that be, Joe-B?

Joe: Oh, couple weeks, I guess.

Engine quits. Tony restarts it.

Katie: You ain't forgot how to write?

Scarlet: No matter how small the parts they
                first offer, you, Anton, grab it. And
                never say "shucks". (Engine quits)

Tony: Shucks. This damn ... (restarts engine)

Joe: Write 'cha every hour, Katie girl.

Katie: As will I, Joe-B. As will I, you know I
                will.

Scarlet: Don't loose heart, Anton dear. All
                those dreams will come true. (Engine
                quits) I'm sure they will.

Tony: Shucks. This darn ... (starts engine).
                You're all gonna see this famous
                portrait (pointing to his face) in the
                papers soon. You buy up 'bout a
                skillion copies, hear? (Revving up the
                old tapping block six, then letting it
                putter) Forgot to tell you, Ma. Didn't
                have time this morn to milk them
                stupid toggs.

Scarlet: My old job back.

Katie: I'll help you, Mrs. Smenelli and I'll do
                all your chores, too, Joe-B!

Joe's face contorts as though he questioned Katie's
sanity, then takes a final glance up at the bedroom
window. One of the curtains is now slightly parted. Within
the unlit colonial bedroom, the elder Smenelli peeks out
from behind a parted lace curtain.

Engine revving about to take off. The boys singing: "Mama, don't let your boys grow up to be cowboys.

Girls: Goodbye! Bye! Bye! Bye!

Brothers: Giddiup, Silver! Up, Scout! Hi, yoo Cookies! Your grannies's underwear! Awaaaya!

With halting jerks, a barrage of backfire, and clouds of smoke, the Smenelli brothers ride off yelping and shouting. In their wake, the girls sadly wave and cough.

Scarlet: Take care (cough), my darlings.

Meanwhile, inside, the elder Smenelli at his bedroom window, releases the lazy lace curtain. It falls into place and he turns sadly away.

As they pass through Hicksville, villagers are drawn to the ruckus raised by the brothers and their sign covered jalopy.

At the other edge of town, the brothers are smiled upon by a bevy of pretty cowgirls seated on a corral fence.

Out on the open road, the brothers look up then wave at a puffy cloud. From the cloud Harpo strums articulately across his harp, then pauses to point down at the brothers and silently laughs his big disarming laugh.

Like early explorers climbing virgin hills and rounding scenic bends, the brothers bounce and rattle along, anticipating what lies ahead. Music is produced magically as Joe, seated atop his seat's headrest, pretends to play his keyboard: "Nothing's gonna stop us now".

The brothers ride away over a distant hill and the music fades off.

*   *   *   *

One morning while driving in heavy outer city traffic, Joe approaches the skyline overlooking a great aerial panorama of the City. Excitedly, he shakes Tony. Tony and Mangy wake and gaze out in wonder at the imaginary land of opportunity and miracles. The exciting disco flair and lyrics describing the Big Apple explode around them.

Soon the brothers inside their old convertible are caught in the midst of snarled traffic in the middle of the Brooklyn Bridge.

Tony: Stop!

Joe: Stop what ... breathing? This car ain't going nowhere.

Tony: This is it! Remember, Joe-B? Sinatra played a sailor who came home. Stopped the cab, got out like this (demonstrating with flair) and sang like this ...

Tony draws a deep breath about to sing, but car horns start beeping. Then two cops grab him.

1st Cop: Come on, get into our squad car.

Moving traffic and honking horns urge Joe to drive on.

Joe:	Hey! That's my brother!
1st Cop:	Move on, Buster. You can see him at the 29th. We want to talk to you, too.
Joe:	(Grimacing) Oh, God.
2nd Cop:	(Hustling Tony away) Who do you think you are... Sinatra?

*   *   *   *

Bustling Broadway. Several aspiring performers dodge and squeeze their way through the crowd — A tall, spectacled music student toting a tuba high on his shoulders — Two confident, black skate dancers and their talented child slipping through — A pudgy actress memorizing her script, walks hurriedly, face sincerely upturned, eyes strained closed, lips moving rapidly, bosom bumping into passerby, startled eyes open and return to her lines, mind on audition — Two harlequin lovers in white face and multi-colored clothing pantomime as hand in hand they skip out from Central Park then stop cars for gratuities. They impersonate a nearby traffic cop, remaining in pantomime as cop sneaks up, surprising, scaring them off.

On foot, and dressed in smart Western garb, Tony suavely carries a dainty attaché while Joe with luggage stumbles over Mangy. Tony helps Joe to his feet and they continue shuffling confusedly through the crowd, soon to become engulfed in a giant throng fighting its way into a towering office building.

The tall tuba player, dancers, actress', mime artists, the Smenelli brothers and Mangy all cram into a tight elevator and pose like frightened puppets stuffed into a travel trunk.

Actress: (To Joe) Why'nt you park 'em bags in-a bus locka?

Joe: I ya ...

Operator: Up!

At the top floor, elevator doors open. The packed-in performers burst out and race to a double steel door bordered by columns. Some of the performers stand stupidly with their noses pressed to the door. All are restricted in movement by their "press-on forward" formation. The wide, tulip lip of the voluptuous tuba reaches far out over their heads and knocks resoundingly on the door. In response, a powerful Ozian voice booms back over the intercom, echoing throughout the hall.

Manager: Who dares knock! How impulsive of you Thin Man with your existential brass spittoon! And you ebony gazelles in leopard print leotards! How presumptuous are you all to expect an interview without an agent's appointment! I command you to find an agent! Be-e-e gon-n-ne!

Glued to each other by fright, the performers and dog rush as one cumbersome lump back to the elevator. Its doors open, releasing a barrage of newly arrived hopefuls who rush for the double steel doors. Without missing a beat, the Smenelli brothers and their inseparable entourage jam into the elevator reassuming their former blank eyed puppet likenesses.

Operator: Going down! (Doors close)

Minutes later, the Smenelli Bros and Mangy are out in the street confronting another towering building. While Joe stands uncomfortably with luggage, Tony studies the address on his letter envelope.

Tony: (Looking up with a confident smirk) Looks to be it.

Joe: Should have came straight here in the first place.

Entering into a small office interior, a stereotype casting agent, squat, balding, cigar-chomping, is seated at the desk unhurriedly interviewing a nervous young hopeful.

Agent: (Art Buchwald/Bernie Stiles scanning a copy of Show business) How you like data? Deb Williams got booked at Jelly's and the Cope. You known I turned her down cold? (Client shakes his head) So, you're not in any the unions, right? (Client nods) Own a car? A trained beagle? Dance? Got a banana that sings?

The office door bursts open! The Smenelli brothers, like experienced ham showmen, exhibit themselves with broad gestures.

Brothers:	Ta-Tanah! Whelp, here we be!
Agent:	Yeah? Who be we?
Joe:	(Stepping forward with big enthusiasm) Well, partner, this super guy's Tony.
Tony:	(Dance stepping up to Joe) And this be Joe-B. We sing...
Joe:	Juggle, do stunts (stands on his head upon the desk).
Both:	We do it all. (Now both are standing on their heads.) The Smenelli brothers! Ta-taahh!
Agent:	(Looking in his appointment book) Smenelli brothers, Smenelli. That name's not in my book, beat it. (To his seated client) Ever work in a cabaret? Bus tables? Shampoo poodles? Anything?
Tony:	(On his feet, going through his pockets) But we have an appointment, Mr. Fishmonger. Here's the correspondence you sent us.
Agent:	I sent you an empty envelope?
Tony:	Well, Pa tore up the letter.
Agent:	Pa tore up your... You guys look too old to have a pa.
Tony:	Swear to God, Mr. Fishmonger.

Agent: Swear to who? Get this guy off my desk! (Joe rights himself) What's God got to do with anything?

Joe: He's got everything to do with EVERYTHING, Sir.

Agent: Who has?

Tony: Ask your secretary. She signed that letter as I recall.

Agent: Oh, she did. Well she's out on her regular all-day lunch break. And your name still ain't in the book.

Joe: (Bending close over the book) You plum sure 'bout that, Sir? (Agent slams book in Joe's face)

Agent: Listen. I checked today's events top to bottom and all of Shirley's cute little notes around the edges. You guys ain't in there! And I wish you weren't out here either.

Tony: Well, sorry to been a bother, Mr. Fishmonger. (Starts to leave)

Agent: (Reaches to a stack of trade papers) Here, take this copy of Backstage. It lists some of the stage and film auditions upcoming last month.

Tony: Thanks.

Joe:	(Raising his hand) Sir. Maybe you got our name spelled sidewise or something.
Agent:	It's spelled S-m-e-n-e-l-l-i right?
Joe:	Kinda
Agent:	Mr. Smenelli.
Joe:	Yep – per.
Agent:	I'm putting you down on my creep list. Make sure you creep out and close the door quietly when you leave, okay?
Tony:	Yes sir.
Joe:	(Smiling) Whelp. Nice talking to you, Sir.

The brothers open door gently. Mangy is seen in the hall guarding the luggage. The Agent waves after them in disgust. As they leave, a carefree, gum chewing bleached blonde enters.

Agent:	If it ain't Shirley! Welcome back from lunch vacation, doll.
Shirley:	Who were them dudes?
Agent:	Who knows? They didn't have an appointment.
Shirley:	Sure they did. Made it myself.

Agent: They're not in the book. See?

Shirley: It's only Thursday, Mr. Fishmonger. You're looking at Friday.

Agent: Thursday? (Turns to client) Then what are you doing here? Beat it, you lying creep. (Client rushes out). He conned me into believing it was Friday. Who knows one day from another around here?

The Smenelli brothers are reading ads in Backstage. Tony turns to a passerby for directions. Later, in a hallway outside the door of another agency, Mangy guards the luggage while the brothers adjust their ties and hats and smile as they burst into the office. They continue in and out of casting offices without success. A small cramped and crowded waiting area of another agency. The Smenelli brothers and others all sit quietly waiting. The mood is waiting, waiting, waiting.

The brothers and Mangy are leaving the Gulf Western building. On the spacious plaza beneath towering offices, their weariness is apparent as they pause to consider their situation. Standing proud but no longer over confident, nor smiling, Tony rips the final page of Backstage and deposits the torn pieces into his satchel held open by Joe.

Nowhere to go, undecided which way to turn, they frown as they look about with a sense of embarrassment and lack of importance. Homeless strangers isolated in a growing crowd of homebound pedestrians, lost for words and sadly confused, they stare.

*   *   *   *

Now in a crowded Manhattan deli-restaurant during the breakfast rush, sitting in a centrally located table, Tony and Joe stare at the bustling entrance.

The waitress Alice approaches.

Alice:	You boys finally ready to order?
Tony:	That hombre we're to meet ain't here yet.
Alice:	What is this? You guys been parked here over an hour. I'll have to call the manager. Oh, yoo, Mel!
Tony:	Joe-B, I think we're 'bout to get the boot. Better order up something snappy.
Joe:	'Bout time. I'm hungrier'n a pregnant grizzly with worms.
Mel:	What's the trouble here, Alice?
Alice:	I've asked these guys to order and.....
Joe:	I'll have a double dump of sausage, four Jerry Colonas, plate of toasted corn biscuits...
Alice:	(Quickly writing Joe's order) Thanks, Mel. (Mel walks off)
Joe:	....dunked in goat's cream, St. John's cocoa and a king cut of slap appie pie sprinkled with parched oats and pine nuts and topped with spoilt milk.

Alice: (Lowers her order pad to study them. They look up smiling shyly). You're out of towners, right?

Joe: (Proudly) Hicksville, Idaho, M'am.

Alice: Right. So I'll let all that corn ball, slap appie stuff slide by this time. We're a very busy restaurant. That's why all our customers read their menus and simply pick a number.

Tony: We usually start breakfast with two plates of sausage, M'am.

Alice: How delightful. (Writing) That's two number eights.

Joe: Can I have crax with mine?

Alice: Crackers?

Joe: No. Crax.

Alice: Jax?

Joe: Jax?

Alice: Cracker Jacks.

Joe: No crax – cracked corn.

Alice: Where you think you are, back on the chicken farm?

Joe: Got any grits?

Alice:	Four blocks down.
Joe:	Chits?
Alice:	Never heard of it.
Joe:	Bits?
Alice:	Okay, Clem, I'll bite. What do you do with bits?
Joe:	You put it between...
Alice:	Oh, Yoo, Mel!
Tony:	You could'a ordered toast.
Mel:	(Rushing) What's the trouble here, Alice?
Alice:	I think we got ourselves another Jack Tickles here. You listening? (To Joe) Okay, wise guy, now where do I put those bits?
Joe:	'tween sliced avocado and tomatoes on a burnt bun, plastered with small curd shepherd's cheese and fishmush, with 'bout dozen or so nice fat, hot chilly peppers.
Mel:	For breakfast?! Alice, what's he talking about?
Alice:	Never mind, Mel. It's over your head. (In order to avoid answering Mel's question, without looking at him she shoves him away.)

Mel:	Then why'd you call ...?
Joe:	And a side plate of ...
Alice:	Hold it! Fortunately, it's pay day. Still, I'm very busy. So, let's play strictly by the numbers?
Tony:	Just bring us anything.
Alice:	No! Not anything! Anything is a word! Like patience! And explode!
Tony:	(Rising) Joe-B, I've gotta go to the out house.
Alice:	No! No one goes to the out house while I'm exploding! (Pushes him back into his chair) I need a number! Like 10-9-8-7...
Mel:	(Rushes over) Alice, what's the...?
Alice:	(Without looking, shoves Mel off) 6-5... you better pick a number before I reach zero.
Joe:	27!
Alice:	Oy vay!
Tony:	Ain't 27 a number.
Alice:	What's this, a fancy restaurant here? We only go up to twelve! Look at your menu.

Joe:

Why're all these big numbers here?

Alice:

(Bracing herself on Tony's shoulder) Listen, Guys. Get your chits and bits together. I'll be right back. (Glances at her watch) Pill time.

Tony:

(Glancing at the entrance) What's this Drummer feller look like anyway?

Joe:

Big Horn said he's an Aussie from Australia.

Tony:

Big Horn?

Joe:

Whatever his name. That there big-tall feller with his tuba we met in the elevator.

Tony:

What's he look like? And don't tell me he's a big-tall feller who likes to show off his tuba playing, busting everybody's ear drums loose in elevators. I was inquiring 'bout this Drummer feller and you knew who I meant. Boy, I sure had it with your silly wise crackers.

Joe:

(Offended, turns his face away) Gosh, Tone. I weren't gonna wise crack ya any. (Covering his face with one hand and crossing his leg) Think I don't see when time's is serious? Think I don't know when you're in no mood to be joked with? Gosh, Tone!

Tony:	(Consolingly touching Joe's shoulder) Sorry, Joe-B. Guess all this waiting's getting to me. Waiting at toll booths, in traffic, on phones, elevators, waiting rooms, for waitresses and appointments like waiting for this Drummer feller. Waiting, waiting, always waiting. Waiting to get to New York. Now I'm here and I'm still waiting.
Joe:	I ain't no bale of hay, you know.
Tony:	Gosh, Joe-B. I meant you, too.
Joe:	It's alright. I understand.
Tony:	(Rubs Joe's hand) Thanks, ole brother. Now what's this Drummer feller look like?
Joe:	(Sigh) Welp, he's an Aussie from Australia, right?
Tony:	Right.
Joe:	So, he'll either be hopping round like a kangaroo or carrying a koala on his platypus.
Tony:	(Gritting) Know what I'd do to your big nose if'n we weren't in public?
Joe:	Tony-Boy. How you gonna face all this waiting and all without a sense of humor?

Outside the deli, a clown dressed in a limp, oversized Kangaroo costume, peers in through the large window. He holds koala and platypus shaped balloons. The word "Dunfy's" on each. After struggling through the revolving entry the kangaroo clown looks about. Tony glances at the entrance and is stunned upon seeing this strange costumed character smiling and waving at him.

Tony: Joe-B. Uh, about that Drummer fella looking like a kangaroo. That weren't a bet was it?

Joe: What's matter with you? Course no.

Tony: Then let's get up to greet him. He's hopping over here right now.

Joe: Hopping?

As the brothers stand, their chairs fall backwards from the weight of their sheepskin jackets. A thin man rushes from a nearby table and helps them to upright their chairs and coats. The brothers thank him and he rolls his bulging eyes, smiles and leaves.

Drummer: Ah! The brothers Smenelli, I presume.

Joe: Howdy. Who ...?

Drummer: Reginald Percival Drummond and you are definitely Josiah, the eldest and least influential of the troupe. And this extremely talented looking visage is surely your soon to be talked about brother Antonio.

Joe: How did ...?

Drummer: Big Horn described both of your attributes concisely.

Joe: His name's really Big ...?

Drummer: Sit. Sit. Sit. (They all sit and stare at each other.)

Drummer: You two seem surprised.

Tony: No

Joe: Not really. No.

Tony: No. No. Just we ain't ever talked to no talent agent from Australia before. Have we, Joe-B?

Joe: Not really. No.

Drummer: Blimmy. There it goes again.

Tony: (Startled) What goes?

Joe: (Looking about) Where?

Drummer: Referring to me as a bloody Aussie from Australia. To all you Yankees, I'm either an Englishman, Canadian, South African or Aussie.

Passing Drunk: Whoa, Ossie! Hey, Buddy, you got a match?

Drummer: Beat it, you Irish lout! (Drunk leaves)

Tony: Then where are you from?

Drummer: Any dialectician can tell immediately by the way I cross my "T's" that I'm a Lemnian.

Joe: Cross your "T's"?

Drummer: A native Lemnian born and bred in dear ole Lemnos.

Tony: And I'll bet you're proud of it, too.

Joe: Where is such a place?

Drummer: In the dictionary, but I see you haven't yet eaten.

Joe: How'd you know such a thing?

Drummer: No crumbs near the cracker bowl. Pickles neatly packed. Not a spot of drippings upon your nappies. Terribly decent of you two to tame temptation not touching these treats till I attend the table.

Joe makes faces in his attempt to form the peculiar "T" sounds made by Drummer.

Drummer: But now that I'm here —- shall we? (Begins eating pickles)

Joe: Ain't we gonna pray first?

Tony: Won't this kinda ruin our breakfast?

Drummer: Breakfast? This is breakfast? Oh, I
            see you haven't yet learned how to
            survive on a performer's meager
            income. Observe the calories, coloring
            agents, bleaching ingredients, etc.
            Not to mention preservatives and
            non-essential additives present in
            that lovely array which has been set
            free before us. Now I add a generous
            jerk of ketchup into this lifeless glass
            of water and Presto! Tomato juice
            appertife.

Tony: (Glancing over at Alice who is still
            taking her pills) You mean we ain't
            gonna order anything?

Joe: (Glancing over at Mel chopping onions)
            Just sit here eating pickles and drinking
            ketchap?

Drummer: Precisely the way to remain solvent
            till we get our show on the road. Oh,
            my, here she comes. But I don't think
            she'll recognize me. Last time I was a
            rabbit having tea with a mouse.

Alice: You guys ready to order yet? And you –
            the kangaroo with the balloons – are
            you supposed to be funny?

Drummer: I've just arrived.

Alice: So what? You gonna order or do I call Mel?

Drummer: If you do insist. We'll have the numeral eight in triplicate simmered casually au jus.

Alice: (Writing) Three orders of sausage in natural juices. (Looks up) You mean in grease?

Drummer: Served precisely at 9:24 when we'll have concluded our business. Is that satisfactory, Madame Garson-ee?

Alice: I'm happy if you're happy. (Exits)

Drummer: Now, Gentlemen, if there are no further questions, let's all sign the contracts and toast our success. I believe someone left a glass of water at the next table.

Tony: Actually, there were some questions we were fixing to ask ya.

Drummer: There's only one question. Are you two really ready to become rich and famous stars gathering admirers throughout the universe? Would a fan club headquartered in the perfumed boudoirs or nobility embarrass you? Might it belittle you to step from your Rolls and strut freely into the palatial sanctions of high society? Repetitiously greeted day in and day out by princesses Grace, Diane, Jackie, Spanky and the whole gang.

Tony: You sure pack a lot into one question.

Drummer:	Confidentially, if I may question your manhood. Are you two men man enough to satisfy an international star's harem? Like Brando, will you find time to enjoy the exotic pleasures of your private fantasy island, where no broad is too keen, no dream too extreme and no competition from Mean Joe Green?
Joe:	A man need only satisfy one woman – his wife.
Drummer:	Is he serious?
Tony:	Yep.
Drummer:	One woman. A wife. And after the honeymoon, the diapers, the jellyrolls and tea, would it have been worthwhile after all? After the screaming, the crying, the bottles and divorce. After they've brought your bald head in on a platter, would it have been worth it after all? After all and after all...
Tony/Joe:	After all what?
Drummer:	After all, you two hadn't come all the way here from Hicksville for marriage, but for stardom. And tonight the golden door to the stars can be open to you. I say this very night, at this address – my card – the most influential names in show biz will be attending a special party given by myself in your honor.

Joe: We don't party.

Drummer: What? You don't party? But his isn't just any party. In fact who said it was a party? How can one call the biggest ball ever held at my pad a party? Rolling Stone would call it an historical gathering of greats. Everybody will be there.

Tony: Everybody?

Drummer: Everybody.

Joe: If'n Hoover Garrison the dogcatcher shows up, I know I ain't going.

Tony: Joe-B. Drummer's talking big names.

Joe: What names?

Tony: What names?

Drummer: What names? Names, names, uh, Streisand, Jaggart, Reynolds, Dick and Liz, Paul and Joana, Frank and Betty, Carson and his former, Collins and her ex. Eddy and Jeanette, Gable and Lombard. Need I go on?

Tony: Wow!

Joe: Yeah, wow! Tone, I'm too scared to go. I wouldn't know how to act or what to say. So why're we going?

Drummer: Contacts! Contacts! Uh, picture yourselves in a self-service market. There you are, undiscovered talent pushing your shopping carts down rows of contacts and opportunities. You stop and say hello to a jar of Lamet. You talk spaghetti to Dino DiLaurentis. Steady a side of beef for Stallone. Throw blood pudding at DePalma. What more do you want from an agent?

Joe: What's a jar of Lamet?

Drummer: You'll have to excuse me. It's nearly 9:24 and I'm turning into a pumpkin. Here are three contracts in triplicate. Choose either plan A, B or C. Then bring everything, including my fee, to the party tonight at nine. We'll finish up there. (Finishes his ketchup juice) Ahh! Remember, important people will be there, thus my reputation will be at stake. So pretend you're somebody.

Tony: I guess we can do that pretty good.

Joe: (Nodding in agreement) Don't forget your balloons. That's a real fancy get up you're wearing there.

Drummer:	How reckless of me not to've mentioned that Dunfy's Distinguished Drivables is opening their new used car lot in the Bronx. They've given me a small part in their commencement festivities. Yet, as you know, there are no small parts. Only small wages. But that's show biz. Tally Ho! (Hops out)
Tony:	Whoa, Golly.
Joe:	Wow! Whoa there.
Tony:	Whoa! Easy. My head's still spinning.
Joe:	Yeah, whoa! Things just don't happen like that back in Hicksville.
Tony:	Whoa, Boy! Ho!
Joe:	Ho! Whoa! Way up there.
Tony:	(Sigh) Whoa!
Joe:	Wowie whoa!
Passerby:	(Leaning close) Hey, man. I can go for whatever you're on.
Joe:	(Looking around) Just my chair. There's an empty seat over yonder. (Passerby leaves)
Tony:	I don't think he was talking 'bout your chair, Joe-B.

Joe: Didn't think so. But I didn't know what
                         else to tell 'em.

An ordinary couple walk excitedly among the
customers, talking loudly as they try selling chances on
the upcoming Oscar winners.

Ann: Hey Jerry! It's him. It's him. We finally
                         found him.

Jerry: Who?

Ann: The guy who won the "Who Shot J.R.
                         Contest"!

Jerry: Sure. That's him. Thank Jehovah. Our
                         prayers are answered. Here, Brother.
                         $250.00 dollars, right?

Ann: We thought we'd never find you again.
                         Go on. Take your winnings with our
                         blessings. It's yours.

Tony: No, M'am. I can't.

Ann: "No M'am"? Ain't that cute how these
                         corner studs pick up on western movie
                         talk?

Jerry: Take your winnings. Please. Her
                         conscience has been torturing me ever
                         since you didn't show up for the pay
                         off. You see, she's a born-again Jew.

Ann: It's only fair. You won your bet. So,
                         grab your money and leave us alone!

Joe: Honest, M'am. My brother really ain't the one you're looking for.

Ann: Then it must be you. Jerry! It's him!

Jerry: Sure. I'd recognize that phony cowboy anywhere. Here's your winnings, Brother. Spend it wisely. From the wisdom of Solomon let me say (holding out the money to Joe) "For I handed on to you that which I also received, that Christ died for our sins according to the Scriptures."

Ann: Jerry, that wasn't Solomon.

Jerry: So, I skipped a few pages. Here, take your dough, Lucky.

Joe: I can't. I'd be dishonest.

Ann: Oh, he's probably just too bashful to appear on the show.

Tony: What show?

Jerry: The Stellar and Moira TV show. You know, Jerry Stellar and Ann Moira. Besides the cash prize of $250.00 dollars the winner of the "Who Shot J.R. Contest" gets to appear on their show.

Joe: Hear that, Tony-Boy? The winner gets on some TV show.

Ann:	Not just some TV show. It's a show all about giving. The sick get healed. Estranged families are reunited. Drug addiction, alcoholism and sins are replaced with love and spiritual drunkenness. Everyone is helped to live a more fulfilling and happier life. Let's suppose one of you wanted to be a star of Hollywood or Broadway …
Jerry:	Come on, Ann. Stop embarrassing these guys. Can't you see they came all the way from out West to enjoy Mel's sausages (picks one up). Hey, Alice! Are these Kosher?
Ann:	Tell the people how it feels to win?
Joe:	But we didn't win. We ain't never won nothing. 'Cept my prize rodeo buckle Tony-Boy's wearing.
Tony:	Sure wish I were that winner. But we never bet, 'cept 'tween ourselves and pappy.
Jerry:	(Looking sadly at Ann. Hugging to comfort) Sorry, Honey. That's the breaks. (They walk off) Anyone wanna take a chance on the stupid Oscars? Winner gets two weeks in Lou Costello's home town of Patterson. But we must have the name and address of you or your nearest relative. Over here, Ann.

Ann's Voice: How long you been at this address, Mrs. Barnaby?

Woman's Voice: Forty-three years.

Jerry's Voice: Now may we see your draft card?

Alice: Here's your three eights, Boys, enjoy.

Tony: How 'bout three more eights, toast and a pot of cocoa. M'am.

Alice exits. Tony and Joe bow in silent prayer, then they begin eating.

Joe: Want I should read you Katie's letter again?

Tony: No. It's kinda depressing to hear all that happy news from back home.

Joe: Specially 'bout how much Katie misses me and all them there weddin' plans.

At the next table, a lone, lovely young woman begins slowly shifting her chair and table closer to the Smenelli brothers. Noticing her strange behavior, Joe contorts his face to indicate to Tony that the girl is probably crazy. Ignoring her, they continue their conversation. But as she, her chair and table come quite close they counter to avoid her by shifting their own chairs and table away. Eventually, the boys are pinned between her and an adjoining table whose occupants observe all and react accordingly.

Joe: And Ms. Prim ate up all Ma's petunias.

Lynn: (The eavesdropper) Who's Ms. Prim?

Tony: An old goat who keeps sticking her nose into everything. Same way you got no business here, Miss.

Lynn: You can hardly make me leave. This is a public place you know?

Joe: Pa warned ya 'bout big-city folk. Pay no 'tention, Tony-Boy. She probably got a blown head gasket.

The brothers shift their chairs closer together and lower their voices. Lynn moves yet closer.

Lynn: Where are you two from?

In a brilliant attempt to avoid the pretty eavesdropper, the brothers bow their heads below their table and whisper. Lynn persistently clings close. Then, in desperation, the brothers drop down out of sight. Finally, all three end up together on their hands and knees under the table, staring stupidly at one another.

Joe: Kinda' quiet under here, ain't it?

Lynn: I couldn't help but overhear you two talking to that advertising clown. I didn't quite understand everything, but I gather you boys are performers seeking an agent.

Tony:	You an agent?
Lynn:	To be perfectly frank, I'm just getting started. It's been my childhood dream to be part of that world of glamorous stars. Joy Todd advised me to first build yourselves. I hope you'll forgive my eagerness to meet you two. I've even had business cards printed. Here (now searching her satchel) I might just happen to have a blank contract handy here somewhere.
Joe:	Plan A, B or C?
Tony:	(Reading card) "Agent for the Stars, Lynn Zarra, Talent Manager". That you?
Alice:	(Peering under the table) Want I should call Mel, Lynn?
Lynn:	No, Alice. We're just having a confidential business discussion. I'll explain later.
Alice:	I met these guys. No explanation's necessary. (Leaves)
Joe:	Excuse me, but my sausages are getting cold. (All three rise and sit at the table)
Lynn:	I'm really sorry to've interrupted your meal.

Tony:	It's alright. Anyway, we already got an agent.
Lynn:	Which isn't the same as a manager. An agent will rarely give you advice, correct any problems, prepare you and pay all your expenses, but I as your manager will.
Tony:	You're still a woman.
Joe:	And Pa always said "Women and business don't mix".
Lynn:	You're kidding.

The brothers grab at the extra servings of toast, sausages and cocoa left by Alice. They are about to bite into sausages sandwiched in toast until Lynn cries out:

Lynn:	Don't you dare bite into those horrible chopped up carcasses of dead greasy pigs!

Their mouths open, about to bite, the brothers are shocked into a freeze pose.

Tony:	What was that, an ad for Alka seltzer?
Joe:	Sure weren't meant to work up the appetite.
Lynn:	It's disgusting. The only desirable morsel at this table is that decorative sprig of parsley.

Tony: Guess we best clear 'way the
                  undesirables then. Joe-B, why'ont you
                  help Miss Zarra outta her chair?

As the brothers rise, their chairs fall backwards again.

Joe: Will do. Let me help you up, Miss.

Lynn: I was only trying to prevent you both
                  from poisoning yourselves. As your
                  manager it's my duty to look after your
                  welfare. (Looking into her satchel) Oh,
                  you haven't signed the Contract.

As Joe picks Lynn up, chair and all, her shoe falls off.
He makes a half-turn with her towards Tony who places a
chair for her to step down on. Joe then picks up her lost
shoe, wrinkling his nose as he hands it to her.

Lynn: Gentlemen. Thanks a heap. It's so
                  nice to know that chivalry isn't dead ...
                  just sick. (Hobbles off angrily on one
                  shoe.)

The brothers smile and wave a cute goodbye.

Joe: Think she might belong to the female
                  Mafia?

Tony: Might. Sure got a suspicious wiggle.

Joe:	(Sits, removes his boot) Her card fits right nice over this hole in my forty-dollar lifetime boots. Just four days hoofing 'round town and lookie there – a peep hole big as the bore of a double 12 gauge.
Tony:	(Lifting his jacket off the floor) My sheepskin's got all dirty. We oughta hang'em on a rack.
Joe:	Best take our wallets out of them first. But it sure won't be comfy wearing a bulge in these tight pants.
Tony:	Joe-B! My wallet's gone!
Joe:	Mine too. Musta dropped on the floor.

They crawl about the floor and end up under their table again.

Tony:	They're gone, Joe-B! Our wallets, all our savings and all are plum gone.
Joe:	Think that nice fella with the kindly eyes who helped pick up our jackets before, maybe wasn't so nice?
Tony:	Don't know. I can't think.
Alice:	(Looking under the table) What's the matter, Boys, indigestion? Seven eights 'll do it every time. Here's your bill. Pay at the door. (Leaves)

Tony: (Reading the bill) $14.84!

Joe: How we pay it?

Tony: Dig down deep, Brother, and let's see
                   how much we can come up with. And
                   pray. It's possible. Just possible.

Joe: Here. Twelve cents. Two McMoney
                   coins and a squashed Snark Bar.

Tony: That female agent!

Joe: You ain't gonna panhandle off some
                   pretty little gal?

Tony: Nope. I rather go to jail.

They rise quickly and see Lynn standing by a far table.
She is gathering her notes, sachet, hat, gloves and dining
bill and preparing to leave. The brothers rush to her.

Joe: Now try to be nice, Tony.

Tony: What was her name?

Joe: Her cards in my boot. Miss something.

Joe/Tony: Oh, Miss! Hold on a minute there,
                   Miss! Yah, Miss! Wait, Miss, please!

Lynn tries to escape them but is overpowered. One to
each side, they lift and carry her back to her table.

Lynn:	What is all this? Let me down. Somebody call Mel! I'm being kidnapped! Won't somebody help! Anybody here from Brighton Beach?
Tony:	(Forcing her into her chair) Shhh. We've reconsidered your offer.
Lynn:	What offer? I wouldn't offer you two stooges a spot in the cleaners.
Tony:	And I want nothing to do with no female agent.
Lynn:	(Quickly rises) Good!
Tony:	(Softly) 'Cept we're broke and can't pay our bill.
Lynn:	(Studies them with pity. Sits slowly) I see. That explains your sudden change of heart towards me.
Joe:	You said if you were our manager, you'd pay our expenses.
Lynn:	I said that? If so, I meant it with certain limitations. Now I'm not sure we can work together. A manager expects, even demands dependability, tact, craft, trust, friendship, long term loyalty. If I sent you to an audition or gave you an assignment, I'd expect you to be prompt, eager and able.
Joe:	Sounds like getting married.

Lynn: Obviously, all you really want from me is a momentary escape from a minor debt. Under those conditions, I must say NO. (Rises to leave, but Tony holds her.)

Tony: I apologize for the way I acted towards you. But it ain't easy for a man like me to accept a bossy female – a man born on a frozen mountainside, a man who's slept with wild animals, (her eyes widen in shock) a man who's rounded up the 'oneriest cows you ever saw, who's worked muddy meadows, sweated morn till night, every night dreaming of that one big shot on Broadway. A sweet, soft gal like you just can't understand a man like me who'd never taken orders from a woman before to suddenly ...

Joe: Oh no? What about Ma?

Tony: Joe-B! Will you hush up? Ma's are differed from women.

Lynn: Oh (picks up their bill), how much is it? $14.84! For what? Fat fried in grease!?! Ah, who cares? (Places money and the bill on the table, gathers her satchel, gloves and puts on her hat then starts away) I'd wish you good luck. But personally men, I don't give a damn.

Tony: (Singing while watching her go) Strangely she came.

Joe:	Touching his chair with her table.
Tony:	Strange as a child's wildest fable.
	Wond-rous is the way of life's game.
	Bright were her eyes, lighting a flame at my table.
Joe:	But you were not eager nor able.
Tony:	(Nods) Sadly I now realize.
	She flows down the deli aisle
	But I still hear her footsteps on my chair.
	Was that a barefoot angel there?
	Now softly she goes.
Joe:	Paying our bill by the window.
Tony:	(Lifting out his arm and sighing) Ahh, there she goes off in the wind blow. So softly she goes from my life.
Brothers:	(Alternating) Soft-ly. Soft-ly, Soft-ly, Soft-ly. Soft-ly.
Tony:	Soft-ly.
Tony:	You know, Joe-B. She was kinda pretty.
Joe:	And nice. She sure didn't have to pay our bill, knowing we'd never see her again.

Tony: Yepper, kinda pretty.

Joe: And nice.

          *   *   *   *

Along 5th Avenue, the Smenelli brothers happen into a crowd gathered around a channel 9 TV interview.

Tony: Joe-B, lookie all them cameras. Gee wilikers, I'll bet they're making a movie right 'chere. Wow! And do I got a brilliant idea how we can get in it. Come on!

During the following interview, our two heroes and a few other show-offs are seen walking to and fro in the background, popping on and off camera. As their confidence gains they do oddly daring and amusing bits. This in accordance to the Ancient Bubonic belief: "By simply being seen on TV, regardless how stupid your actions, you will somehow become discovered and immortalized.

Newscaster: (Woman newscaster) We are talking to Dorothy Clark on the location of the movie "They all Laughed", co-starring Ben Gazzara and Audrey Hepburn.

Dot: (Bending to mic) And John. Don't forget to mention sweet, marvelous John.

Newscaster: Dorothy, with the recession putting a bite on big budget films, will the studios continue to produce vehicles of this magnitude in the future?

Dot: Why ask me or anyone about the future? Only God knows, right?

Newscaster: Off the top of your head, what do you guess will happen to highly paid performers such as yourself, Audrey and Ben?

Dot: (Bending to mic) And John. Don't forget to mention...

Newscaster: Magnificent, precious John, yes. What I'm really asking is would you stoop to wait tables, clean out cruddy barns and so on if times got that hard in the industry?

Dot: Hard times? Huh? Performers are used to starving. If the economy went all the way down to absolute zero, most of us would hardly notice. It would be like old home week. I see they're all set up to shoot again. I better go. (Starts away) Oh, hey! If you want to bore your viewers with more idle chatter come along to the party tonight!

Newscaster: Thanks, Dorothy!

In the background, Tony goes all the way in giving tribute to the first Bubonic boob by doing a terrific one arm handstand on smiling Joe's head – certain immortality. Unfortunately, the police move in and the brothers are knocked down and shoved off camera in the swift shifting of the crowd.

Tony: (Sitting on the ground) Hear that, Joe-B? Audrey Hepburn, Ben Gazzara and Miss Clark are all coming to our party tonight.

Joe: And John. Don't forget that fellar John.

Tony: Drummer boy sure knows his way 'round town.

Joe: I'll bet anyone, what he don't know ain't worth knowing.

Tony: Hey! That camera man is waving us to come over to the set. Come on!

As the brothers run onto the set, their fellow show-offs gather outside the police barricades and watch.

Tony: (Bogie tough) You call us?

Joe: (Giddy) Welp, here we be. Ta-dahh! (Turns and smiles and waves back at the curious crowd.)

Gaffer: Did you guys know ...

Tony: (Mean faced, rough voiced) Pal, anything we don't know, ain't worth knowing.

Gaffer: ... know that a camera hog is the dumbest looking, lowest form of life that ever existed?

Joe, oblivious to all but his admirers, continues to wink, nod and smile at them.

Gaffer: And the next time I spot you two on this or any other set I'll have you locked up! Got me?

Tony: (Hanging tough) Gotcha. Come on, Joe-B. We got things to do.

With a proud, affected strut, Tony leads Joe away. Joe still ignorantly nodding, waving, smiling and winking at the remaining crowd. The brothers leap and flip over the barricades amid cheers. After getting their hands shook and their backs slapped, the brothers bid farewell and leave their fellow buffoons, who continue waving and smiling.

Joe: Adios, Buckeroos! Have to go see our hairdresser or something! (Turns) Where are we going, Tone?

Tony: (Pressing forward, tough and determined) You don't pay 'tention too much, do you?

*   *   *   *

AUTHOR'S NOTE

The adventure has just begun...

In the next installment our protégés, The Smenelli brothers, meet up with Lynn Zara, a talent agent for her struggling NYC agency: Even Dogs Have Talent.

She finally arrives at a catchy and proper name for the rag tag western band of wannabes the brothers picked up along the trail to the Big Apple – FIREBRAND!

This is just one of the many adventures, along the Yeller Brick Trail.